'WOW' IS ' UPSIDE DOWN

Ed Reardon

AuthorHouse™
1663 Liberty Drive
Bloomington, IN 47403
www.authorhouse.com
Phone: 833-262-8899

This book is printed on acid-free paper.

Interior Image Credit: Sarah Legere

ISBN: 978-1-6655-6624-7 (sc)
ISBN: 978-1-6655-6625-4 (e)

Library of Congress Control Number: 2022913800

Print information available on the last page.

Published by AuthorHouse 07/22/2022

author HOUSE

A Mother has an important and very special job

She is blessed and honored in the sight of God.

She nurtures and cares for her children
with love in her nest,
She sings songs, and holds them gently;
she always knows what's best.

A loving, tender voice and skin so soft and nice,
She is more wonderful than sugar and spice.

She is more precious than diamonds or gold,

This is the truth, this is what the Bible has told.

A Mother who loves Jesus is more than a friend.

She is one on whom you can always depend.

Busy as a bee and sometimes on the run;

She still sets time aside for her kids to have fun.

A Mother who loves the Lord is a gift from above.

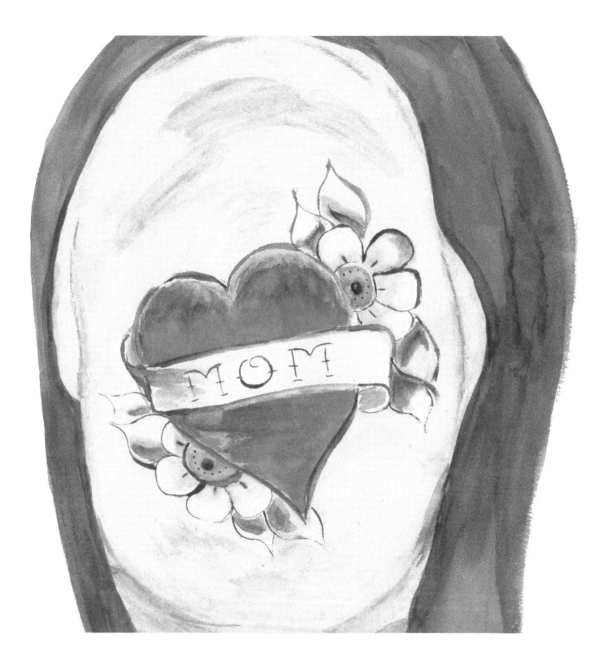

She, by nature, reveals God's love.

You'd like it if she was always happy,
but sometimes you make her mad.

Just remember she always loves you,
even if you did something bad.

A boy or girl should give honor to their Mother.

Give her a kiss or call her up and
tell her that you love'er.

She desires the best for her kids
whether they are grown up or new;

She's the one who is anointed by
God, to be the mother for you.

She is like a doorway or connection
between Heaven and Earth.

God created a life and she brought forth a birth.

If you are adopted because you needed a home,

It took a step of bravery to call you her own

'WOW' is 'MOM' upside down if
you turn it around that way.

Let's give thanks to our Mom each and every day.

CPSIA information can be obtained
at www.ICGtesting.com
Printed in the USA
BVHW022243030922
646238BV00026B/425